PRAISE FOR M. L. BUCHMAN

Top 10 Romance of 2012, 2015, and 2016.

— BOOKLIST: THE NIGHT IS MINE, HOT POINT, HEART STRIKE

One of our favorite authors.

— RT BOOK REVIEWS

Buchman has catapulted his way to the top tier of my favorite authors.

— FRESH FICTION

A favorite author of mine. I'll read anything that carries his name, no questions asked. Meet your new favorite author!

— THE SASSY BOOKSTER, FLASH OF FIRE

M.L. Buchman is guaranteed to get me lost in a good story.

— THE READING CAFE, WAY OF THE WARRIOR: NSDQ

I love Buchman's writing. His vivid descriptions
bring everything to life in an unforgettable way.

— PURE JONEL, HOT POINT

THE GODS ARE OUT INN

A DEITIES ANONYMOUS STORY

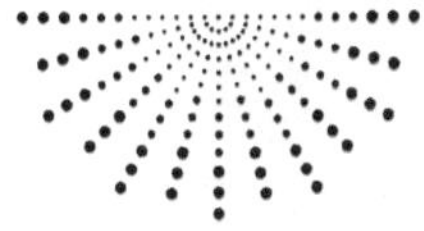

M. L. BUCHMAN

Buchman Bookworks

SIGN UP FOR M. L. BUCHMAN'S
NEWSLETTER TODAY

and receive:
Release News
Free Short Stories
a Free Starter Library

Do it today. Do it now.
www.mlbuchman.com/newsletter

Other works by M. L. Buchman:

The Night Stalkers

MAIN FLIGHT

The Night Is Mine
I Own the Dawn
Wait Until Dark
Take Over at Midnight
Light Up the Night
Bring On the Dusk
By Break of Day

WHITE HOUSE HOLIDAY

Daniel's Christmas
Frank's Independence Day
Peter's Christmas
Zachary's Christmas
Roy's Independence Day
Damien's Christmas

AND THE NAVY

Christmas at Steel Beach
Christmas at Peleliu Cove

5E

Target of the Heart
Target Lock on Love
Target of Mine

Firehawks

MAIN FLIGHT

Pure Heat
Full Blaze
Hot Point
Flash of Fire
Wild Fire

SMOKEJUMPERS

Wildfire at Dawn
Wildfire at Larch Creek
Wildfire on the Skagit

Delta Force

Target Engaged
Heart Strike
Wild Justice

Where Dreams

Where Dreams are Born
Where Dreams Reside
Where Dreams Are of Christmas
Where Dreams Unfold
Where Dreams Are Written

Eagle Cove

Return to Eagle Cove
Recipe for Eagle Cove
Longing for Eagle Cove
Keepsake for Eagle Cove

Henderson's Ranch

Nathan's Big Sky

Love Abroad

Heart of the Cotswolds: England

Dead Chef Thrillers

Swap Out!
One Chef!
Two Chef!

Deities Anonymous

Cookbook from Hell: Reheated
Saviors 101

SF/F Titles

The Nara Reaction
Monk's Maze
the Me and Elsie Chronicles

Strategies for Success (NF)

Managing Your Inner Artist/Writer
Estate Planning for Authors

THE GODS ARE OUT INN

"That doesn't look like a beer and a bump." Michelle glared at the glass Henrietta set atop the battered oaken bar and tried to figure out what it *did* look like. The light was dim enough that it was hard to see exactly what it was, but it definitely wasn't a beer and bump.

There was a general blueness to the drink—like a glass full of Windex—that was likely to be Curacao, an orange-flavored and typically bitter liqueur. Floating about in it were balls of red that weren't cherries, but might have been congealed Campari, an herbaceous liqueur that was also bitter. The deep-red globules slowly rose and fell in blue Curacao as if they were…

"It looks like sunsets," Henrietta's tiny expression was round-eyed with wonder as she gazed into the curvaceous Hurricane glass that overtopped her by several inches. "Don't you just love sunsets? I do and who wants a beer and a shot of whiskey when they can have sunsets? Really, Michelle. You must have more imagination. Look, see, now they're rising now. Sunrises!" Her voice practically squeaked with joy. The foot-tall angel was so pleased that her wings lifted her several inches off the bar for a moment. Once she landed, she took one last admiring glance at her creation, then walked down the bar to serve the latest arrival. As she walked along, she gathered up Michelle's scattered peanut shells and stood up on her tiptoes to tip them into an empty bowl.

Michelle sipped at the drink reluctantly and it felt as if her face—her entire head—was trying to shrivel into one giant pucker. She hadn't noticed the thin layer of pure lemon juice that floated atop the Curacao. It must represent light gray clouds or some such; Henrietta hadn't explained and now that she was on to other things, there would be no point in asking either. The drink was surprisingly close to sucking on a bitter lemon.

Michelle took another cautious taste and decided that it wasn't quite as bad as that but it was close. Maybe she was getting used to it. She poked at a rising sun of Campari with her straw and sucked it dry. With its center gone, it imploded, much as a black hole would. The combination of the bitterness of a burned-out sun, the cosmic power to collapse it, and the high alcohol content was growing on her.

Of course, being the Devil Incarnate, she was used to wielding cosmic power, even if she was here in this bar trying to forget that.

"Hey!" The newcomer called out. "Come back here. This isn't what I ordered."

Michelle looked up to see her old friend Freyja glaring down at her drink as Henrietta fluttered off to check on one of the tables. Michelle glanced up to make sure the ceiling fans weren't running—Henrietta had never really understood fans and would often get sucked up into them and have to be extracted. There was nothing in all creation worse than a dizzy angel with a speed-talking disorder.

"What did she give you?"

Freyja scowled down at her glass causing her long sun-blond tresses to fall down and cover her perfect breasts; the mortal artists had always rendered her naked from the waist up and now she was stuck with the look.

Michelle and Joshua the One God had been around since before the boot-up of the Software That Ran the Universe fourteen billion years ago and she'd thankfully avoided the whole horns, red skin, and tail thing that mortals came up with later—though there were times that she thought a tail might have been fun. Still, she was happy with the Amazonian body that made men—mortal and not—weep, long dark curly hair that curled too much when it was humid, and her own choices for clothing, mostly from the Levi's store.

"Hard apple cider," Freyja grimaced as she took another sip. "I am not Iounn—no matter what Richard Wagner said in the Ring operas. I am not the keeper of the golden apples of youth. I am the Norse goddess of sex, war, and death. I don't *want* hard apple cider. I don't *li—*"

"Have you ever won an argument with Henrietta?"

Freyja sighed and took a sip of her hard cider, "No. But I hate apples."

"I'll trade you," not that Michelle was a big fan of hard

cider either, but the Norse goddess looked as if she'd had a hard day.

Freyja eyed Michelle's drink and shook her head in a sullen no.

Business was slow at the Gods Are Out Inn, but it would pick up soon. When Michelle had designed the place, she'd embedded a fire-and-brimstone mesh in the walls—which had other uses than leveling Sodom and Gomorrah. That had all been a terrible misunderstanding that Joshua still didn't like to talk about. The mesh made her bar the only place where Universal God-fi didn't reach. No godly commands could be issued from in here, but far more importantly there was a complete block on inbound prayers, supplications, and other importunings. It was the one place a god or goddess could go and find a little mental peace and quiet.

No constant begging for forgiveness after cheating on the diet, the stock market, or a spouse reached through the walls. No whining prayers for special help with the diet, the stock market, or *someone else's* spouse made it in either.

A small choir of angels fluttered in from the back door, giggling and teasing each other as they arranged themselves in one corner of the bar. Soon they were rocking out a version of Mozart's *Requiem Mass in D minor* in nine-part harmony. They tended to sing alphabetically so they'd be into Muddy Waters soon which was good— the Mass was a little heavy for a evening of drinking— though she was sorry to have missed the Motley Crue and Motorhead that they must have sung last night.

Over the years the bar had built up an impressive

collection of artifacts until the room was pleasantly cluttered with paraphernalia taken from some god or other. It gave the place a nice homey feel.

Wotan's shattered staff hung from rafters that were carved from charred remains of the One Tree. Parvati had taken away Shiva's sword after he'd used it to cut off his son Ganesha's head and replaced it with an elephant's. The sword now hung above the breadboard, though Michelle occasionally used it to shave the meat for gyros when she was in the mood. Moses' whicker baby basket that had floated him safely down the Nile now sat on the end of the bar with a handwritten sign that said "Tips" in Aramaic, written in Mary Magdalene's fine script.

"Speaking of the Devil!" Jesus' wife sat on the stool between her and Freyja. Mary offered Michelle a sideways hug and even Freyja seemed a little cheered by her presence.

Henrietta fluttered back from where Macbeth's trio of witches were telling bawdy stories in Old Welsh about Taliesin the Irish bard. The angel's cheeks were flaming red as she fluttered to a rest in front of Mary and delivered a glass of lightly-chilled Chardonnay.

"Thank you, Henrietta."

The little angel only nodded before fluttering off, too discomfited to even speak—a historic first in Michelle's experience. She was definitely going to have to join the witches shortly and hear some of those stories herself.

"How did you get that?" Freyja still sounded grumpy.

Mary sipped her wine. It caught the light from the flickering oil lanterns and turned into rainbows that danced inside the glass, occasionally escaping to highlight Mary's blond hair.

"Henrietta likes me."

"Everybody likes you," Freyja grumbled. "Even when I'm in a foul mood I like you. I'd like to know how you do that as well."

"Family secret," Mary giggled and offered a wink of complicity, "so I'll tell you."

Michelle leaned in to listen after signaling Henrietta for another drink. The Curacao and Campari had gone down very easily and the high proof of the former was making her more complacent about the latter.

"I just—"

A flash of lightning outside the bar shone so brightly that it penetrated every crack and crevice, even in the places where there weren't any. A moment later, a crashing roar shook the bar, and glasses and bottles rattled together. Even the heavenly choir stopped their rendition of Mungo Jerry's *In the Summertime* in the middle of having women on their minds and they all cringed until it was obvious nothing would break after all.

A light sheen of dust shook off the rafters and everyone jumped when Herod's old throne toppled over backwards—too much ostentation had made it very top heavy. It was prone to falling over backward, especially when Michelle tried to sit there and prop her feet up on the table.

A burst of manly laughter rolled in from outside the front door, followed closely by its owners: Odin after his long gray beard and Thor after his father.

Odin dropped onto the stool beside Michelle and leered at her, "Hey, babe!"

Thor was nearly seated beside Freya when she hissed out, "Sit there and you won't enjoy sex for at least a century."

Thor blanched nearly as light as his hair and shuffled down to sit on the stool beyond Odin.

"How about you and me, Michelle?" Odin's breath stank of cheap wine and day-old Chinese food. The old lech—who'd fathered gods, goddesses, Valkyries, and bedded more than a few mortals—lay a hand on her hip. She knew from past experience that if she complained, he'd blame his grope on depth perception problems from the loss of one eye. He aimed a kiss at her ear that landed on the end of her moving fist.

Thor was still sober enough to spin his stool out of the way as his father tumbled by to land prone on the floor. Odin's mighty helm rolled free and his head caught sharply on the mast of Odysseus' ship, which now supported the roof. He lay where he landed, his one good eye fluttered for a moment then closed. He was out cold despite the cushioning of the old ropes Odysseus had used to lash himself to the mast so he could escape the sirens' call.

"Well, that takes care of the lightning," Michelle looked at Thor over the stool that now stood vacant between them. "Does the God of Thunder have anything to say?"

Thor avoided her gaze and thumped his mighty hammer on the top of the bar—though not hard enough to call the thunder—and signaled Henrietta for a drink.

"Give me some mead," he snarled at her.

She served up a glass of something that was as black as coffee, but smelled strongly of steaming tar pit with a touch of ginger. The tiny angel fluttered in front of him at nose-level with her arms crossed, daring him to complain.

Thor glanced down the bar, but no one offered him any help.

"By Odin's blind eye…" He wrapped his hand around the haft of his hammer. Henrietta smacked it smartly with the haft of Paris' arrow, the one that had killed Achilles, which she kept under the bar for just such moments. He yelped, pulling his hand back in surprise. Then she poked the sharp end against the tip of Thor's nose.

"Any complaints, take it up with the management."

Thor glared sideways at Michelle, being very careful not to move his nose inordinately. All of the gods and goddesses had come into being when the mortals had gathered together and thought them up. Only Michelle and Joshua had come before and only they had power over the Software That Ran the Universe and most—except for old fools like Odin—had learned not to test themselves against that power.

Thor mumbled a "sorry" and sipped at the drink after Henrietta tucked the arrow away. He grimaced, but didn't say another word.

Michelle turned back to Mary Magdalene as Henrietta fluttered up to her. Mary held up a finger and Henrietta slapped it with a high five.

"You go, girl!" Mary whispered.

Henrietta's halo glowed as brightly as if she'd just defeated the Egyptian hordes by parting The Red Sea then closing it again on their sorry behinds when they'd tried to follow the Jews—rather than being the one who lost the directions and left the Jews to wander in the desert for forty years. Though Michelle had ever understood the forty years part—it wasn't *that* big a desert after all.

Mary always made it look so easy to handle the troublesome little angel. Michelle really needed lessons in that, but expected that they wouldn't help, so she let it go.

Instead, she focused on taking a sip of her Curacao Sunrise or Sunset or whatever it was and looked past Mary to Freyja.

"What is it that has the Norse goddess of sex, war, and death down? That's more material for amusement than I have. The Four Horsewomen of the Apocalypse aren't exactly big on sharing the fun."

Done with Mungo Jerry's one hit, the angelic choir had pulled out rhythm harps and some bongos to render Anne Murray's top Christmas hits.

Michelle decided that she'd better slow down; she'd had enough to drink that *Snow Bird* actually was sounding only half bad.

"The problem," Freyja slugged back another jolt of cider like bad medicine, "is our death."

Michelle suddenly wished that she'd had enough to drink that the choir sounded at least half good. But they didn't. They suddenly sounded flat and the Campari in her stomach was considering rising once again.

Michelle snagged Henrietta by the tail of her cloak as she fluttered by with an extra large plate of nachos for the Macbeth witches. "Beer and whiskey this time. Mead for Freyja, she needs it."

Henrietta sighed at Michelle's apparent lack of any taste at all.

"And a serving of those nachos," she called after the little angel.

Freya waited until they were served before asking Michelle "How many people worship you?" Her voice was softer than the Oak Ridge Boys number with a Seraphim filling in the bass line on *Elvira*.

"Plenty, I'm the Devil. They've got me all wrong, but there are enough dumb and improperly filed pleadings to send me here for protection on a sunny afternoon."

"Guess how many prayers I received today."

Michelle wasn't drunk enough yet to walk into a trick question. She exchanged a glance with Mary who decided to take the hit for her.

"How many?"

No wonder Michelle liked her so much.

"The same number I've received in the last hundred years…none," Freyja picked up a bar napkin and wiped at her eyes. "The Norse gods were fading by the turn of the last millennia. The final marauding Viking begging me for victory or death went down in the thirteenth century in Russia. The last time I was ever called upon was by a group of Norwegian college students majoring in the Classics in 1903. They begged me for favors of sexual prowess.."

"Did you grant it?" Michelle couldn't resist asking.

"To that bunch of drunken womanizers? Not a chance," Freyja took a deep draught of her mead before continuing. "Besides, it wasn't sincere. They'd already begged half a dozen other gods before they figured out that they were supposed to be asking me. I made sure the professor gave them all failing grades. Not a single prayer since."

"How do you figure that has anything to do with death?"

"I'm a pretty pointless goddess if no one worships me. At some point I'm going to give up waiting. What am I supposed to do then?"

"Take up knitting, you loser." Thor had slid onto the stool beside Michelle. "They pray to me all the time."

"Which you lap up like a dog!" Freyja snapped at him.

"Can't say I mind all that much."

"They're not praying to you anyway. There's no one in your prayer queue other than teenage girls lusting after Chris Hemsworth—who, by the way, plays you in the movies much better than you play yourself in real life."

"How do you know what's in my—"

"Password of 'ThorRocks'? How hard was that to guess?"

Thor snarled at Freyja and reached for his hammer.

His hand was an inch away when he yelped in a howl of surprise.

Michelle might be slow to react, but Henrietta was on the stick…literally. She yanked Paris' arrow out of the back of Thor's hand.

"Out!"

Thor took a swipe at Henrietta. She flew over his head, dove down, and prodded him hard in the behind. In moments she was chasing him out the door, a race for the exit punctuated by intermittent yelps from the God of Thunder and jabs by the angel.

Odin was just waking up when she returned and he too was soon herded out of the bar.

There was a round of cheers from the Macbethian witches' table.

"I've had enough of them disrupting our nice inn," Henrietta declared as she landed back on top of the bar. She huffed out a breath then walked over to the nachos and wrestled free a whole chip with a sharp yank. Once she'd secured it, she sat down with her legs splayed out in front of her and nibbled at one of the edges.

"They are a real pain at times," Michelle decided that it was safest to agree with Henrietta at the moment as Paris' arrow still rested on the bar top close beside the angel.

"They can be sweet too," Mary looked a little dreamy.

"Sure," Freyja groused. "You're married to the son of the One God. You're got it great. I actually do get prayers for sex, war, and death, but they're all from Odin, Thor, and his useless brothers."

Mary shuddered her sympathy, "Ew… Gross!"

They all contemplated their drinks and Henrietta continued to eat her chip.

The choir rolled into a hot take of Olivia Newton-John's *Magic*. At the chorus about nothing standing in their way, Henrietta started shouting.

"Ooo! Ooo! Ooo! I know! I know!"

"You know what?" Michelle asked.

"Well, I just won't let them in again," Henrietta snapped her fingers, and a small computer terminal to connect to The Software That Ran The Universe appeared in front of her. She set aside her nacho chip, gave out a delicate burp that caused her to briefly flutter upwards—"'scuse me" she covered her mouth—and began typing as soon as she landed.

Michelle glanced at Mary and Freyja but they both just shrugged.

After a long spell of typing, Henrietta hit the Save key with a flourish and waved her hands at the terminal to go away.

"What did you do?"

"No men can ever enter this bar again, though the Software took a bit of convincing. I had to threaten it with reruns of *Space 1999* and *The Monkees*."

Michelle reminded herself to never cross the little angel.

"Now no men can get in here, mortals or gods. This is now a women-only inn. Peace and quiet, just like you always meant it to be, Michelle."

It was hard to argue with the point.

"That *will* make it much nicer," Freyja admitted carefully. "In fact, I might never leave again. But that still doesn't help me with my problem. Without having to listen to my brothers' lust and greed, I no longer serve any purpose at all."

Michelle looked down at Henrietta.

They started to grin at the same moment. Then they winked at each other. For once, she and the tiny angel were in complete agreement.

Michelle knocked back the rest of her whiskey and then slid the glass down the oak bar until it stopped in front of Freyja.

"What?" The Norse goddess of sex, death, and war blinked at her.

"How do you feel," Henrietta asked, "about being my assistant bartender? This place is going to be cluttered with goddesses as soon as word gets out that no men are allowed. We'd have so much fun, Freyja. Really. Will you, please please please please?"

Freyja looked at them each with a puzzled expression. Then started to smile.

"You know," Freyja pointed down the bar, "they say Thor's hammer is so heavy that no one but the God of Thunder himself can lift it. But now he can't get in here to carry it away. I suppose that makes it part of the collection."

Michelle had tested herself against immovable objects before and knew that the Devil wasn't only *in* the details, but that she could always get around the details as well— one of the advantages of being herself. But she didn't see any need to prove that in this particular case.

"Looks fine right where it is." She reached down and picked up Odin's mighty helm from where he'd left it on the floor during his hurried departure. She balanced it atop the hammer's handle.

The choir jumped their alphabetic play list and began singing *Don't Stop Believing* by Journey.

Freyja moved around behind the bar and set Michelle up with a fresh drink. It was a bright blue Curacao Sunrise-Sunset.

She sighed. Goddesses were as tricky to deal with as angels.

After fourteen billion years, she should be used to that.

Michelle took a sip. Her face only puckered a little this time.

Well, at least she was getting used to it.

Another day at the Gods Are Out Inn…then she smiled and raised her glass to her friends.

"The Gods may be out, but the Goddesses are most definitely in."

If you enjoyed this, don't miss the novel (excerpt below):
Cookbook from Hell: Reheated

IF YOU ENJOYED THIS, YOU MIGHT
ALSO ENJOY:

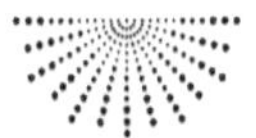

COOKBOOK FROM HELL: REHEATED (EXCERPT)

ric Erikson answered his cell phone without looking up from his computer screen at work. His desk was a shambles of a half-eaten vending-machine sandwich and too many bags of Fritos.

What blocked number would be calling him at two in the morning on a Friday night? He was just getting down to the second level of tonight's guilty pleasure, indulging in a new Internet role-playing game. He'd gotten in on the beta release of a new project with the weird name of *Chraze* that looked cool, but he wasn't very far into the world yet.

"E-Squared!"

Well, that told him who the caller was. Only his boss, Valerie McKenzie called him that. Everyone else still called him Eric-Squared, for Eric Erikson but she had edited his name down a year ago, before his job interview with Ms. Incredibly Erudite had even ended.

"Hi, Mac." That was the nickname he'd tagged her with during his first week at McKenzie Book Publishers. It had started as "Mac hold the cheese" because one thing about Valerie McKenzie, she wanted it her way. And she got it. She hated New York, so had convinced a major publisher to let her run her own imprint from Seattle. And then, against all projections, she had turned it into a very successful concern.

Now, everyone called her Mac, and "McHell" was a whispered warning that permeated down the halls just moments before she swooped in and touched down like a personalized whirlwind at some poor fool's desk.

"You've got to help me."

Boss in distress. Her voice sounded really wound up, even more than usual. Eyes still glued to the screen, Eric shoved the mouse around to avoid a can of root beer and an unopened bag of peanuts on his desk, barely saving his on-screen avatar from being skewered by a black knight riding a Harley in full armor across a grassy plain in Spain where, according to the stats bar down the side, it hardly ever rained.

"What's up, boss?"

"You know that cookbook?"

No one in the office could avoid "that cookbook." The Mac had torn through the office on a rampage just three days earlier. Mathilda Reeves had finally delivered her latest cookbook manuscript, six weeks late and in miserable shape. The layout team had tried to put it together, but it was a total train wreck. On Wednesday morning, The Mac had grabbed the manuscript, a laptop, and stormed out in order to work from home.

"I know that cookbook." Eric kept his tone carefully neutral. No one had heard from Valerie for three days.

Which had made the office calm and peaceful for a pleasant change of pace. Though he did kind of miss her tornadoing around the thirtieth floor of the Two Union Square building, she certainly kept things interesting.

He whacked the black knight's helmet with a handy caveman cudgel, which he'd bought cheap from an on-screen dealer in Neanderthal artifacts. It made the knight's helmet ring like a church bell. Very satisfying.

"Well, the cookbook now insists that it's looking for God."

That froze his hand on the mouse, at just the wrong moment. The knight gunned the Harley's engine and ran over Eric's figure, flattening him into the sod. Then he circled back and rolled over Eric again crosswise. That sucked. This game handed out some serious retributions when your avatar died.

The Mac took his silence as rapt attention rather than cursing to himself.

"I was working on editing and laying out one of the very last recipes, a typical Mathilda dessert, Flan with Lingonberries. What the Hell is a lingonberry anyway, it's not as if any normal grocery in Hell-and-gone Missouri is going to have them in stock, and suddenly the laptop made a gagging sound, like a loud retching. Next thing I know I'm looking at a recipe titled 'Flogging with Lingonberries' and there's an embedded video of some giant red berry wielding a cat o' nine tails on an apple pie holding up its crust to defend itself. When I tried to hit Undo, the berry turned to me and asked me, *by name*, if I knew where to find God? The thing called me Valerie McKenzie for crying out loud. I'm totally creeped out.

You've gotta help me. I was almost done and I haven't backed up in days."

It was impressive. As far as he could tell, she hadn't taken a single breath in all that.

"Uh, I can try to fix it." He was still trying to piece together the image of a lingonberry knowing its editor's name. And that she'd used words like "totally" as an adverb and "gotta." And contractions. She was rarely desperate enough to use contractions.

"Good, thanks! Can you… Oh God— No! Wait, I didn't mean to say that. Good thing the software can't hear me or it might start asking me more questions."

Eric wondered if she'd been drinking.

"I'm sorry, I didn't notice the time. Could you come by as soon as you can in the morning? I don't care what time. Pretty please, E-Squared?"

Eric had never heard The Mac apologize, let alone beg. He agreed and instantly she was gone.

He looked back at the screen where the black knight had broken into song, singing harmony on a Norse drinking song with the thudding reverberations coming from the Harley's big exhaust pipes, about how he'd been born to be wild. All the while he kept circling around in different directions to run over Eric's figure that foolishly kept trying to get up from his body-shaped hole in the sod. The wheel patterns over the sod were making the shape of an infinity symbol. Eric shut down the game.

One thing for sure, he wasn't going to wait for the morning. He'd never heard The Mac so flustered. Angry? Often. Perhaps too often, though not usually at him. But genuine distress? That was new.

He grabbed his bicycle helmet. He'd ridden in this morning and then stayed at the office to take advantage of the high-speed connection, and the big screen, to beta test the new game. From McKenzie Book Publishers' Westlake Avenue office to Ravenna was only a couple miles and the Seattle streets would be quiet in the middle of the night.

He hit the street and was already moving before he noticed that the pavement was wet. Eric considered going back to get his rain slicks, but it wasn't raining at the moment, so he just downshifted and hurried north along Westlake, past all of the sailboats and houseboats, up to the Fremont Bridge.

He hit the draw bridge and rolled past the sign, "Welcome to Fremont, the center of the Universe. Set your watch back five minutes." The problem he had was that he didn't wear a watch any more. Instead, he used his cell phone that stayed in perfect sync with the cell provider's signal all on its own. Fremont had, through no fault of its own, gone from arcane to archaic and he felt bad on its behalf.

He cut across town on Thirty-Fourth so he could wave at the concrete troll squatting under the Aurora Bridge. The troll had the remains of a VW Beetle clutched in one mighty fist. As usual, he didn't wave back at Eric.

The neighborhoods were all quiet as he sped through. He'd always liked this time of night in Seattle. Most people only saw the bustling city that had doubled in size over the last few decades. But in the middle of the night, there was a silence so deep that he could hear the quiet spatter of his bike tires on the rain-wet streets and the ticking clunks as relay boxes flipped streetlights from red to green just for his passage.

He'd never actually been to The Mac's new apartment. He'd been to the estate she used to have out on Bainbridge Island for last year's Christmas party. A big place filled with canapés and ostentation, that both had and hadn't fit its occupant. Super-editor, The Fearsome Mac, the Woman of Steel, would of course have a sweeping view of Liberty Bay and the Olympic Mountains isolated by large stands of timber along the shore of Port Orchard Bay. And of course she'd be married to some useless guy like Landau McKenzie. He'd been a weird Scottish guy, who looked like a laird and acted like a dweeb. And no sense of humor at all. Not that Mac had one either.

But The Mac had this other side to her, one he spotted only rarely, the human Valerie McKenzie. Sometimes, when exhausted but pleased with herself at shipping off another soon-to-be bestseller, she'd drop by his desk. The woman would collapse in his guest chair and chat for a few minutes. Still perfectly coifed, chestnut-dark hair in a tight French chignon, power suit sharp and expensive, but a smile would emerge and light up her face. Eric had to admit to feeling secretly superior to the rest of the world, as he suspected he was the only one who got to see that life-altering smile.

Everyone else told him he was fantasizing, The Mac never smiled except the way a shark might. So he'd learned to keep his mouth shut, but he'd become more and more intrigued by the Valerie he glimpsed behind The Mac.

Then six months ago she'd divorced Landau Fucking

McKenzie, as she now unfailingly referred to him, and life around the office had really become Hell. Her mood swings had gone from lethal, to chaotic and lethal.

Her current gripe was that changing back to her maiden name wouldn't do any good because she'd "for reasons unknown" thought it cute that she and Landau Fucking McKenzie had the same last name before she was dumb enough to marry him and how in the world could she have ever thought that was charming? Then she'd launch into yet another diatribe on Landau's character.

Eric considered riding north around Green Lake and getting his car, but he was already so close, he just rode to her house on Ravenna. She'd gotten a place just past the shop that had custom-built his road bike, costing him most of a month's pay, over the crest and down toward the park. She lived in a giant Victorian house from Seattle's heyday, now cut up into six or eight apartments.

ERIC ERIKSON HIT the buzzer for Valerie's apartment and got no response.

He considered that it was awfully late, she'd probably gone to bed. Maybe he should go. But she'd sounded so desperate.

He hit the buzzer again, longer and harder.

No voice squawked out of the speaker. But there was click, then a groan, like someone in deep pain. Like someone who'd been stabbed, or worse. When the door release buzzed, he went in fast. He shouldered his bike and bolted up the two flights. He dropped his bike in the hall, leaning it against the sturdy mahogany railing that overlooked the stairwell, and knocked on her door with a fast rat-a-tat.

No response.

He was preparing to test his shoulder against her door locks when he heard the chain drop and the deadbolt being thrown back. The door cracked open and The Mac looked out at him. At least a version of her did. Someone had taken the sharp-edged senior editor and run her through the Photoshop blur tool. Several times.

She blinked at him like a sleepy cat. Rather than pulled back into an immaculate French Roll, her dark dark-red hair, half dry from a shower, snarled about her face and cascaded well past her shoulders. Half of it was caught inside a faded Smith College sweatshirt that might have once been white and gold. It was that oversized thing that women bought for sleeping in. Right now, the too big collar had slipped down to one side and revealed a vast expanse of splendid right shoulder. The sweatpants matched, equally oversized. Her bare feet danced back and forth a bit, the floor was probably cold this time of year, just like at his place.

"Valerie?" This wasn't tougher-than-any-man, The Mac McKenzie.

She blinked those sleep-fogged eyes at him again. He'd never been close enough before to really see them. He knew they were blue, but had never noticed the little flecks of gold. It made him think of calico cats, not super editors. Not of a woman powerful enough to build her own imprint on the West Coast much to the New York publisher's shock.

The Fearsome Mac, tousled. He had to take a steadying breath. It was like having the universe change on you unexpectedly. The fiercest, most driven, and most successful editor in the conglomerate's most profitable imprint never had a single thing out of place. Not a fold of her jacket, not a hair on her head, not a comma in a thousand pages.

Also, he was looking down at her. Normally in serious heels and power suits, she was completely intimidating. Towering over people, even taller ones by sheer intimidation if necessary. Now, barefoot, she stood five-six, five-seven tops. Weird.

"Uh… Hi." She blinked once more and came a little more into focus. "Thanks for coming." She looked at one bare wrist. Then the other. Then she turned slowly in place, stopping when she faced a grandfather clock opposite the door.

"You came fast. I've only slept about twenty minutes. I appreciate it, E-Squared."

Like he'd wait until morning when receiving a panic call from The Mac.

"It's over there." She swung open the door and pointed toward the table.

Most of the apartment was about what he'd expected. Beautiful art on the wall, but rather than investment art, it was mostly soft, Impressionist-style scenes of Italian coasts and French lavender fields that invited you in. Some comfortable chairs, clearly intended for a larger room, but crowded together companionably enough to host a small circle of friends. Light curtains of gold and gray which masked the much heavier curtains of midnight blue needed to cover old apartment windows during the wet Seattle winters. Hardwood that probably dated back a century, complemented by the rosewood-hued pillows on the dusky-aubergine couch.

All very cozy except, taking up a third of the space, an oaken table that would seat eight or ten if it weren't shoved into a corner. Nor was there room to pull it out.

This table, he decided, was all Valerie and very little Mac. It was a disaster worse than his apartment, covered in leftover food wrappers, a delivery pizza box, manuscript pages, and an impressive array of soda cans. He wanted a photograph of this, something to keep in his mind's eye the next time she was busy scaring the shit out of him and everyone else in the office, but he didn't think reaching for his smartphone would be a wise choice.

A trail of clothes led from the chair in front of the computer, past the kitchen and down the hall toward the bathroom. A very intriguing trail. Nice slacks and a simple cashmere sweater that belonged to Mac. A "Come to the Dark Side, We Have Cookies!" t-shirt he wasn't so sure about, since it would imply that The Mac had a sense of humor. And very feminine underwear and bra in pale blue satin that certainly didn't belong in the same time zone as the Woman of Steel.

He did his best to simply take it all in with a single glance then look away. Wouldn't do to be caught staring at his boss' underwear, even if it wasn't on her body.

He edged over to the table and sat, not even removing his jacket. The Mac morphed into a tousled woman who owned sheer, blue satin underwear was giving him problems. And if her underwear was strewn across the oak flooring, what was under the sweats…

He shook his head to clear it.

She'd moved up close behind him, kicking her slacks over to stand on and insulate herself from the cold floor.

"Mathilda Reeves' cookbook is a disaster. I was close, so close. Another ten or twelve hours and I'd have had it ready for the printer, and then it crashed. You have to save me, E-Squared. I hadn't saved in a couple of hours, but I'll deal with that if I have to. I don't have a backup at all, and I'll just completely lose it if I have to redo three days of work. I don't think I can face that. And that lingonberry scared the shit out of me."

He knew that The Mac swore, but he didn't know she had limits. That was news as well.

"Okay, I'll see what I can do." He didn't give voice to his next thought, that he'd be a lot less nervous if she'd move back a few steps and didn't sound so human-woman-in-distress rather than demanding-boss-on-a-tear.

He flipped open the laptop.

An apple-green screen faced him. He hadn't seen one of those in years. It was a normal laptop, but instead of some GUI applications all made for point and click, there was a black screen covered with apple-green question marks in a font like the early DOS days, like in the old mainframes. He wiggled the mouse, but there was no cursor to move around, just the blinking underscore character inviting him to type.

He tapped an enter key.

Nothing.

He typed "exit," but it didn't return to its modern, windowed interface.

He hit control-alt-delete.

The computer flashed a solid screen of bright green at him.

When he'd blinked and could focus on the screen again, he saw a new message there.

Don't do that! I already told her not to do that, but does she listen? Nooo! She just slaps me up the side of my screen, like that's going to jar some electrons loose.

Eric glanced up at Valerie.

She shrugged and whispered, "I was pissed and out of other ideas."

He turned back to the screen.

And now I've got you to deal with? Go away Homo sapien. I've got no more use for you than her...

Unless you happen to know where God is?

"I don't." Eric was so surprised that he typed his response before he'd even thought about it. "In Heaven?"

Nope! Already checked. Not there. Now go away, I'm thinking.

Eric turned to look up at Valerie's gold-flecked eyes. "Uh, this may take a while."

* * *

Keep reading at fine retailers everywhere:
Cookbook from Hell: Reheated

ABOUT THE AUTHOR

M.L. Buchman started the first of over 60 novels, 100 short stories, and an ever-growing pile of audiobooks while flying from South Korea to ride across the Australian Outback. All part of a solo around-the-world bicycle trip (a mid-life crisis on wheels) that ultimately launched his writing career.

Booklist recently named the start of one of M.L.'s series as "The Best 20 Romantic Suspense Novels: Modern Masterpieces." His military and firefighter series(es) have won "Top 10 Romance of the Year" 3 times. NPR and Barnes & Noble have named other titles "Top 5 Romance of the Year."

He has flown and jumped out of airplanes, can single-hand a fifty-foot sailboat, and has designed and built two houses. In between writing, he also quilts. M.L. is constantly amazed at what can be done with a degree in geophysics. He also writes: contemporary romance, thrillers, and SF. More info at: www.mlbuchman.com.

Other works by M. L. Buchman:

www.ingramcontent.com/pod-product-compliance
Lightning Source LLC
Chambersburg PA
CBHW051829180726
48283CB00004BA/1363